SKYLANDERS UNIVERSE

The Mask of Power

Stump Smash
Crosses the
Bone Dragon

GROSSET & DUNLAP
Penguin Young Readers Group
An Imprint of Penguin Random House LLC

Written by Cavan Scott
Illustrated by Dani Geremia—Beehive Illustration Agency

ISBN 978-1-101-99503-7   10 9 8 7 6 5 4 3 2 1

The Mask of Power

Stump Smash
Crosses the
Bone Dragon

by Onk Beakman

Grosset & Dunlap
An Imprint of Penguin Random House

About the Author

Onk Beakman knew he wanted to be a world-famous author from the moment he was hatched. In fact, the book-loving penguin was so keen that he wrote his first novel while still inside his egg (to this day, nobody is entirely sure where he got the tiny pencil and notebook from).

Growing up on the icy wastes of Skylands' Frozen Desert was difficult for a penguin who hated the cold. While his brothers plunged into the freezing waters, Onk could be found with his beak buried in a book and a pen clutched in his flippers.

Yet his life changed forever when a giant floating head appeared in the skies above the tundra. It was Kaos, attempting to melt the icecaps so he could get his grubby little hands on an ancient weapon buried beneath the snow.

Onk watched open-beaked as Spyro swept in and sent the evil Portal Master packing. From that day, Onk knew that he must chronicle the Skylanders' greatest adventures. He traveled the length and breadth of Skylands, collecting every tale he could find about Master Eon's brave champions.

Today, Onk writes from a shack on the beautiful sands of Blistering Beach with his two pet sea cucumbers.

Chapter One

Missing

S tump Smash was having a bad day. All the Skylanders were. It was a day they thought would never happen. Could never happen.

Master Eon had disappeared.

No, it was more serious than that. Master Eon had been kidnapped—spirited away by agents of Kaos, their archenemy and the wickedest soul Skylands had ever produced. The Skylanders had no idea where Master Eon had been taken. They weren't even sure how it had happened—although they had some very nasty suspicions.

As he stomped through the echoing corridors of the Eternal Archive, Stump Smash replayed the events in his mind. The Skylanders had been searching for the eight Elemental fragments of an ancient weapon known as the Mask of Power. They were still a little unsure what the Mask of Power actually did, although legend suggested it could make its wearer all-powerful. Kaos was also searching for the fragments, and had managed to get his evil little

hands on the Tech piece already. Fortunately, the Skylanders had beaten him to four of the other fragments, guided by the Book of Power and Other Utterly Terrifying Stuff (Vol. 3).

The book was held right here in the Eternal Archive. Or, at least, it used to be.

The book had gone missing, along with Master Eon. Only a Portal Master could read its pages. A Portal Master like Master Eon. Or Kaos.

At least Kaos hadn't managed to reach the fragments that the Skylanders had already collected, thought Stump Smash as he strode through the archive's vast vaults. The Water, Air, Earth, and Undead pieces were safely locked away. Nothing could get them.

"What do you mean Kaos got to them?" Spyro the dragon spluttered as Stump rounded a corner.

Spyro was standing openmouthed, staring at a large robotic figure in disbelief. Chief Curator Wiggleworth was a Warrior Librarian, the protector of thousands of powerful books here in the archive. Like all Warrior Librarians, he was an imposing figure, towering over Spyro in a suit of gleaming mechanical armor. At the heart of the suit squirmed Wiggleworth's true form, a tiny and incredibly old bookworm who was also one of Master Eon's most trusted friends.

"I don't know what's happened," Wiggleworth said. "No one should have been

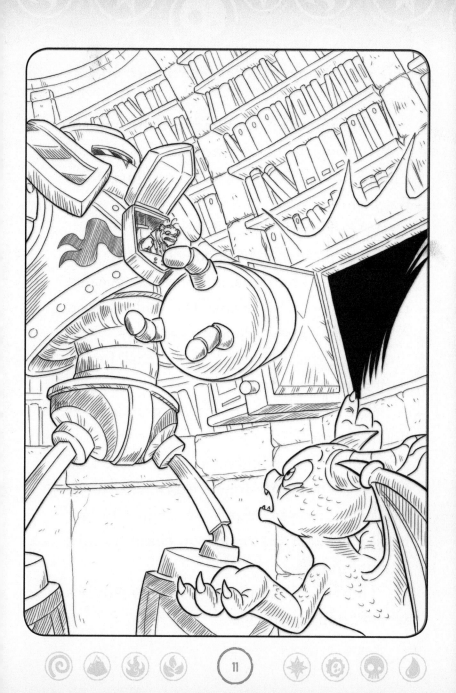

able to open the vault except Squirmgrub or me—"

"Squirmgrub," rumbled Stump Smash, interrupting the conversation. "The Warrior Librarian you assigned to help us guard the fragments."

Wiggleworth's head drooped.

Squirmgrub had been one of the curator's most trusted librarians, until he was revealed to be an agent of Kaos. He had spirited Master Eon away to goodness-knows-where and stolen the fragments of the mask for his dark master.

"He was a traitor," Spyro growled. "A double agent."

Stump Smash had never seen Spyro look so angry. The purple dragon was many things. Adventurous, yes. Impulsive, definitely. But he always kept his temper in check. Unlike Stump himself.

This time was different. Spyro's red eyes were burning with rage.

"Don't you see, Wiggleworth?" Spyro said. "This means Kaos now has five of the eight fragments." The dragon turned toward the open safe. "We should never have stored them here. We should have taken them to Master Eon's citadel. They would have been protected there."

The curator shrugged, his mechanical shoulders whirring. "But Master Eon said . . ."

"Master Eon is gone," Spyro snapped, whirling around. "Because of you!"

Stump Smash raised his mallet-like fists, trying to calm the situation. "Spyro, this isn't helping . . ."

The dragon turned on the Life Skylander. "But we let him down, Stump. We let Master Eon get captured."

"We didn't even know he was in danger," Stump insisted.

"We should have! We're Skylanders. We protect Skylands. That's what we do!"

"That's what we were doing," Stump

reminded him. "We were busy, and Kaos struck—but we'll find Master Eon. I promise."

Spyro took a deep breath, his raised scales relaxing slightly. "I know," he said finally, nodding. "Have we heard from the others?"

Stump Smash wished he was bringing good news. He shook his trunk. "Lightning Rod and Zoo Lou are searching Fantasm Forest. Scratch and Flashwing are on their way to Molekin Mine."

Spyro sighed. "It's taking us so long now that we can't use the Portals."

"Yes," muttered Wiggleworth. "Well, we can't use them without . . ."

His voice trailed away as Spyro shot him a look. "Without a Portal Master," the dragon said in a voice that was frostier than an ice-clops's snow cone. "Yes, we know."

Another voice echoed around the chamber. "Spyro, where are you?"

It was Flameslinger, a Fire Skylander and

one of Stump Smash's oldest friends.

"Over here, Sling," the powerful tree called out.

Flameslinger tore around the corner before skidding to a halt in front of them, a red-hot trail sizzling in his wake. The elf was always on the move, rushing here, there, and everywhere. He wasn't one for cooling his heels. Behind him, a smaller, short-legged figure struggled to keep up. This was Hugo, Master Eon's right-hand Mabu. The little fellow was a natural worrier, but he had impressed Stump Smash since Master Eon had vanished. Stump had expected the Mabu to fall to pieces, but Hugo was rising to the challenge, helping coordinate the search for the missing Portal Master.

"We've got a problem," Hugo said, huffing and puffing as he joined the others. "I mean, another one."

"I'm not going to like this, am I?" Spyro sighed, sharing a look with Stump Smash.

"Well, you told us to listen for anything weird," said Flameslinger. "And this sounds pretty weird to me."

"What does?" asked Stump Smash.

"It's the Giggling Forest," Hugo replied, peering over his glasses. "Spyro, it has started to cry."

Chapter Two

The Weeping Forest

"Okay, run it by me again," said Flynn. "There's a forest that laughs?"

"We've explained this twice already," Flameslinger snapped. He was holding on to the edge of the hot-air balloon's jiggling basket.

"Hey, hot stuff," said Flynn the pilot, grinning and pulling a lever, trying to ignore the fact that it had come off in his hand. "I've been kinda busy here, trying not to crash."

"That's a first," grumbled Flameslinger under his breath.

Stump Smash understood the elf's

frustration. As soon as Spyro had heard about the Giggling Forest, he had dispatched Stump and Flameslinger to investigate, along with the Tech Skylander Countdown and the Magic Skylander Wrecking Ball. They'd called upon Flynn to transport them to the forest in his hot-air balloon. Flynn was Skylands' best pilot. They knew this because Flynn was always telling them. He'd pointed it out three times before they'd even taken off, and twice more since nearly smashing the basket into the Eternal Archive's tallest turret. The Mabu was almost as full of hot air as one of his balloons, but he'd helped them many times over the years. There was a good heart beating in that puffed-up chest.

"The clue's in the name, Flynn," Stump said. "The Giggling Forest giggles. All the time. It has done it for thousands of years."

"What's the joke?" Flynn asked, spinning the wheel to just avoid a school of sky-salmon . . . only to find himself heading straight for a flying whale.

"No one knows," Stump replied, stumbling into Wrecking Ball, who had wrapped his tongue around the ropes to stop himself being flung from the basket. "I guess they're just happy."

"Not anymore," pointed out Countdown. "What's-his-name said they started crying."

"Flameslinger!" The elf laugh, before shrugging at Flynn. "Don't mind Countdown, he gets forgetful."

"Do I?" asked Countdown. "I can't remember."

Wrecking Ball snickered, but couldn't join in the conversation. He was a little tongue-tied, after all.

"This isn't good," said Countdown. "This isn't good, at all."

They were standing in the middle of a clearing in the Giggling Forest, after making what some would call a bumpy landing. Flynn was calling it awesome, but he was also trying to rebuild the basket that had "accidentally" smashed into the ground. The pilot also claimed that someone must have raised the island by a few yards at the last minute, but the Skylanders were too taken aback by the sound greeting them to argue.

The trees of the Giggling Forest weren't just crying. They were wailing.

"Stump, you better talk to them," said Wrecking Ball.

"Why me?" asked Stump Smash.

"Because you're a tree?" suggested Flameslinger.

Stump Smash couldn't argue with that. He marched forward to the nearest blubbering trunk.

"Hey, what's up?" he asked, trying to get the tree's attention. "Feeling a little blue?"

The tree stopped sniveling for a second,

looked at Stump with watery eyes, and then bawled. "We're so sad," it howled, sap streaming from its wooden nose.

"We kinda noticed," said Countdown, walking up beside the Life Skylander. "But what's wrong?"

"You'd better see for yourselves." The tree sniffed, waving them farther into the forest with a trembling branch. "It's awful."

The Skylanders cautiously made their way through the teary trees. Flameslinger even slipped a fiery arrow into his bow, just in case.

Something dreadful must have happened here.

And then they found out what.

"Whoa," said Wrecking Ball.

"Unbelievable," breathed Flameslinger.

"That's something even I won't forget," said Countdown.

Stump Smash could see why. A gigantic crater, carved deep into the ground, stretched out in front of them. All around, the trees nearest the blast site were standing still. They weren't laughing. They weren't crying. They weren't making any sound at all.

Countdown tapped against the trunk of one tree with one of his hand-missiles. The sound wasn't the dull knock of metal against wood, but the cold, hard sound of metal hitting rock.

"They've been petrified," the Tech Skylander said, gazing from one statue-like tree to another. "All of them—turned to rock."

"And that's not all," cried out Wrecking Ball, throwing himself forward. He rolled down the crater and up the other side. "I was right," he called. "Come and see."

The Skylanders rushed across the blackened earth, stopping in amazement when they reached Wrecking Ball.

Stump Smash's eyes narrowed and his lip curled into a snarl. "Trolls," he growled. They were everywhere.

Stump Smash despised Trolls. Long ago, he had been a normal tree, happy to sleep his days away in the middle of a peaceful glade with his brothers and sisters. But then the Trolls came.

They chopped down his forest to use as fuel for their weapons. Not even Stump Smash had escaped unscathed. They'd stripped his branches, leaving him with two giant mallets.

It was a decision they soon regretted. Stump Smash went on a rampage— smashing the Trolls' lumberjack equipment, before starting on the Trolls themselves.

But things were different this time. He didn't need to smash these Trolls. They weren't going anywhere. Wrecking Ball rolled over to the nearest Troll and flicked out his tongue.

"Ugh," Flameslinger shuddered. "Do you have to lick it?"

"It's rock," Wrecking Ball confirmed. "Just like the trees."

"They all are," Countdown agreed, checking out a petrified Troll Greasemonkey who was frozen in position, a giant wrench held high above his head. The look on his face was one of sheer terror.

"These aren't normal statues," said Flameslinger, taking a peek from beneath the blindfold he always wore. "They used to be real."

"Just like the trees," Stump Smash muttered. Even after all this time, he found it hard to feel sorry for a bunch of Trolls. "But how did this happen to them?"

"Is someone there?" came a voice from deeper inside the stone forest. "Can you help me?"

"I recognize that voice," Stump Smash declared, rushing forward and knocking over a petrified Trollverine that shattered into a thousand pieces on the rock-hard ground. "Come on!"

"Please, somebody help me!"

"We're coming," Stump Smash replied. "But I wouldn't count your lucky stars just yet."

The Skylanders crashed through the trees and found the owner of the voice cowering beneath a stone bush.

"Glumshanks!" cried Flameslinger, not believing his eyes. The lanky Troll sighed, his pointed ears drooping as he realized who had come to his rescue.

"Oh," the Troll said quietly. "Skylanders. My day just gets better."

Glumshanks had known the Skylanders a very long time—but they were hardly friends. The lanky Troll was Kaos's butler, sidekick, and all-around toady. He'd helped his master on every last one of his despicable schemes, and—despite being treated horrendously over the years—he stuck by Kaos no matter what.

"If you're here," snarled Stump Smash, "then Kaos can't be far away!"

Beside the Life Skylander, Countdown's bomb-like head was starting to flush scarlet—which was never a good sign. "Yeah, where is the little twerp?"

Glumshanks shook his head. "Oh no. I'm not going to betray Lord Kaos."

Flameslinger pointed a flaming arrow at the Troll. "Then you better start running!"

"Can't do that, either, I'm afraid," Glumshanks answered, crossing his arms across his thin chest.

"Too scared?" Wrecking Ball said with a grin. "Know that we'd catch you anyway?"

Glumshanks looked down at his feet, his usual hangdog expression dropping even further. "Not exactly."

The Skylanders followed his gaze and their mouths dropped open. Glumshanks's legs had been transformed into stone.

Chapter Three

Glumshanks's Story

"What happened here?" growled Stump Smash.

"I've told you," Glumshanks insisted. "I'm loyal to Lord Kaos."

Wrecking Ball sniggered. "Like he's loyal to you?"

Glumshanks sniffed. "He's never let me down yet."

"And I thought I was the one with the bad memory," said Countdown, before nudging Flameslinger in the ribs. "I am the one with the bad memory, right?"

"Okay, fair's fair," said Stump Smash. "I

suppose we better get you free."

Glumshanks looked as amazed as Stump Smash's fellow Skylanders. "S-seriously?" he stammered. "You're going to help me?"

"Sure." The Life Skylander nodded and flexed one of his mallets.

"It's my legs," Glumshanks pointed out. "They've been turned to stone." Stump Smash looked down at the Troll's long legs. Sure enough, they were now pure rock, fused into the stone around his petrified toes.

"That is a problem," Stump Smash admitted, giving one mallet fist a little practice swing, "but one I'm sure I can hammer out."

Glumshanks's eyes went wide. "Hang on a minute . . ."

"You better stand back a bit guys," Stump Smash told the other Skylanders. "We don't know how hard this stone is."

"What are you going to do?" Glumshanks shrieked.

"Smash your stone-ified legs, of course," Stump Smash said, before turning to Wrecking Ball. "Is stone-ified even a word?"

"I don't know." Wrecking Ball shrugged. "We could ask Master Eon." The Magic Skylander glared at Glumshanks. "Oh we can't, because Kaos has kidnapped him."

"Never mind," said Stump Smash, sounding the happiest he'd been all day. "It won't take a minute."

The Life Skylander raised a gigantic mallet, ready to swing it down on Glumshanks's stone legs.

"No, no, no!" Glumshanks wailed, throwing up his hands. "Please don't clobber my legs. I'm rather attached to them."

"Thing is," Stump Smash said, hammer still held high, "I reckon Master Eon would know how to get you free without smashing your shins into sand."

"If only we knew where he was," added Flameslinger, his burning arrow still ready to fly.

"Okay, okay, you win!" yelled Glumshanks. "I'll tell you everything. I promise."

"Then you better get started," Stump Smash said, a satisfied grin spreading over his trunk. "From the beginning."

His ears drooping lower than ever, Glumshanks sighed. "It was the Book of Power."

Wrecking Ball's eyes went wide. "The book did this?"

Glumshanks tut-tutted. "Of course it didn't. It's a book. How could it turn living creatures into stone?"

"I'm a tree," growled Stump Smash, hefting his mallets. "How can I pulverize Trolls?"

Glumshanks giggled nervously. "Of course, good point. No, the book told us to come here, to the forest."

"Had it located the next segment?" Countdown asked.

Glumshanks nodded, continuing his tale. "Lord Kaos sent in the lumberjack Trolls and they cleared the forest with typical efficiency . . ."

"FOOOOOLS!" yelled Kaos, slapping his own forehead in frustration. "What have you done?"

A Troll wearing a ridiculously large helmet and an eye patch scratched the back of his neck.

"Um, clearing the forest as requested, sir," he said, not quite sure why his Lord and Master was shouting at him. "I remember it distinctly. 'Clear the trees to the east of the island,' you said. Here, I marked it on the map."

The Troll, who went by the name General Disaster, brandished a tattered chart of the Giggling Forest, complete with a big cross in red crayon and the words CUT TREEZ 'ERE!

Kaos's face turned a funny color. "Glumshanks!" he shrieked.

Glumshanks slunk forward

and examined the general's map. "Ah," he said, "I think I see the problem."

The butler plucked the map from the general's hands, turned it the right way around, and then passed it back to the confused Troll.

"Oh," said the general. "I was holding it upside down, was I?" He cleared his throat. "Lord Kaos, I regret to inform you that we have cut down the trees on the wrong side of the island."

"IDIOT!" yelled Kaos. "Can't you even tell your east from your west?"

"Well, the trees did keep laughing at us, telling us that this was the west side. But we thought they was just trying to trick us. Sneaky things, trees. You're always saying that yourself, sir."

"One day," Kaos screamed, shaking his fists with fury, "I'm going to sell you all to a Troll-eating ogre and replace you with Greebles!"

"I wouldn't do that, sir," said the general.

"Greebles are even stupider than we are. Everyone says so. Even the Greebles."

"Shut up, FOOL!" Kaos said, jabbing a finger toward the general. A spark of bright light burst from the end of his finger and the general vanished in a sudden blaze of energy. "I hope you enjoy the Outlands. Watch out for the saber-toothed sheep!"

The wicked Portal Master took a moment to indulge in some evil laughter (his third favorite pastime after shouting at Glumshanks and trying to take over Skylands) and then turned his attention to his Troll army. "All right, listen up you feeble excuses for minions. We're going to walk to the other side of the island and try again. Glumshanks, you'll have to carry me."

"Really, Master. It's not far . . ."

"SILENCE!" Kaos boomed back. "From this point on you can only speak when I, KAOS, decree it. Carry me, FOOL!"

Shaking his head, Glumshanks turned and allowed Kaos to jump on his weak back.

"That's better!" screamed Kaos. "Quick, MARCH!"

As the army of Trolls made their way through the forest, news of what had happened on the west side of the island started to spread among the trees. And the trees' snickers gradually turned to sobs.

"It won't do you any good, Kaos," said a rich, deep voice from behind the Portal Master.

Kaos turned, pulling on Glumshanks's ears as he twisted to face Master Eon, suspended in a cage between two hulking Drow.

"What was that, you old fool?" Kaos crowed, grinning horribly at the elderly wizard. "Something to say?"

"You will never win," insisted Master Eon, gravely. "That is all."

"Like I'd never be able to steal the fragments of the mask from the Eternal Archive, or kidnap the mighty Eon?"

Glumshanks nearly fell over as he tried to carry the bragging villain. "To be honest, Lord

Kaos, Squirmgrub did all that," he pointed out.

"And I managed to grab the Book of Power," the traitorous Warrior Librarian added from behind the Drow.

"SILEEEEENCE!" screamed Kaos. "The next person who contradicts Kaos gets Portalled into the middle of Scolding Soup Creek, understood?"

"Don't worry. I'll just Portal them back," warned Master Eon.

"Ah, but you can't," Kaos jeered. "Not while you're in the Nullifying Cage of Power Nullification. You couldn't even Portal a flea, let alone a babbling, treacherous minion. You are helpless! You are at the mercy of KAO–"

SPLAT! Kaos had gotten so excited that Glumshanks lost his balance, sending them both splashing facedown into the mud. When Kaos finally forced himself back up, his features were hidden behind a mask of dark brown sludge.

Master Eon sat back in his cage and chuckled as Kaos berated his bungling butler.

Before long they were off, trudging across the island. Soon they reached the place the Book of Power had revealed: a ring of giggling trees surrounding a large flowering bush. Kaos had taken one look at it and groaned. That many trees could only mean they were searching for the Life Element. Of all the Elements, he hated Life the most— mainly because it was so closely linked to trees. Kaos had never trusted trees. He always thought they were plotting against him. Then again, he thought everything was plotting against him—including his own clothes!

"This is it!" shrieked Kaos. "The Life fragment must be buried beneath these very trees. General Disaster—get chopping. I want every foolish tree gone NOW!"

No one moved.

"Where is that idiot?" screamed Kaos. "Didn't he hear me?"

"You banished him to the Outlands, Lord Kaos," reminded Glumshanks. "For being a fool."

Kaos looked as if he was ready to start pulling out his hair, but luckily he stopped himself before he remembered he didn't have any. Instead he clicked his fingers and recalled General Disaster from his exile.

"General, I need these trees gone, pronto. Break out the Lumberjack Machines of Dooooooom!"

General Disaster looked around. "Where are the Lumberjack Machines of Doom, sir?"

A vein began to pulse on Kaos's forehead. "Glumshanks, did you forget to remind me to remind the Trolls to remember to bring the Lumberjack Machines of Doom from the west side of the island? DID YOU?"

"You didn't tell me to remind you," Glumshanks argued, preparing himself for a banishing.

"I CAN'T BE EXPECTED TO REMEMBER EVERYTHING!" Kaos bellowed. "Write this down."

He waited for Glumshanks to root out a pen and notebook from his robes.

"Rule number one: Lord Kaos is never wrong," Kaos dictated. "Rule number two: I must remember to remind Lord Kaos about everything. Even if he hasn't told me what it is that he needs to be reminded about."

Glumshanks looked up from his notes.

"But how am I supposed to do that . . . ?" he began, only to be shouted down by his master.

"NO QUESTIONS! Rule number three: Always refer to rule number one or get banished into the belly of the nearest leviathan. UNDERSTAND?"

Glumshanks nodded sadly.

"Excellent. Now, General, how do you suggest we solve our little problem?"

The Troll scratched the side of his nose. "You want these trees cleared?"

"I do."

"Immediately?"

"If not sooner."

"No problem." The general grinned, revealing a row of gapped teeth that resembled gravestones. "Not when I've got this."

The general pulled a large round metal device from behind his back.

"Is that a bomb?" Glumshanks asked, swallowing loudly.

"It's the Time Delay Blastificator. The most powerful bomb I've ever created. Biggest. Explosion. Ever." The general pressed a button on top of the device. "All I have to do is click here to arm it."

Kaos's face drained of all color. "And how long is the time delay?" he asked, his voice wavering.

A look of confusion passed over the general's face. "Oh yeah. I knew I'd forgotten someth—"

The Time Delay Blastificator exploded.

Chapter Four

Bone Attack!

"And the general's bomb did all this?" Countdown asked in hushed tones. "That's impressive, even by my standards."

"Oh no," said Glumshanks, looking around at the petrified trees. "This is the handiwork of the thing the general's explosion unearthed: the thing that had been buried beneath the forest's floor for thousands and thousands of years."

"What was it?" Flameslinger asked, equally wrapped up in the story.

Glumshanks shivered at the very thought of it.

"Well?" prompted Stump, knocking his mallets together in encouragement.

Glumshanks opened his mouth and . . .

"ROAAAAAAAAR!"

The Skylanders looked at Glumshanks and Glumshanks looked at the Skylanders.

"Did you know he could do that?" Countdown asked Wrecking Ball.

"Throw his voice?" replied the grub.

"Yeah!"

"I don't think it was him," Wrecking Ball said as a shadow passed over them.

"Oh no," whimpered Glumshanks, looking up into the sky. "Not again."

Stump Smash followed the Troll's gaze and his hammers dropped in amazement.

Soaring high above them was the largest dragon that Stump Smash had ever seen. But the creature wasn't covered in leathery skin or thick scales. It was made of gleaming white bones, and a pair of blazing red eyes burned deep in its ridged skull. Ivory wings beat the air as it swooped around and fell into a dive, rushing toward them.

"Let me guess," Stump Smash said as he stared up at the monster's huge teeth. "The general's bomb unearthed a giant bony dragon?"

Glumshanks nodded. "And an angry one at that."

"Anything else you haven't told us?" Flameslinger asked, letting off an arrow that shot up into the air but passed through the dragon skeleton without even slowing it down.

The dragon opened its mouth and breathed out a blast of laser breath. The dark energy struck Flameslinger's bow, knocking it from the elf's fingers. He gasped as he snatched the weapon back up from the ground.

"No!" he exclaimed. "It's been turned to stone."

"So that's what happened to the trees," said Stump Smash. He ducked as the dragon swept low over their heads before zooming back up into the sky again.

"And the Trolls," Glumshanks said as glumly as his name suggested. "The horrible creature shot up from the crater before the smoke had even cleared and started petrifying everything that moved."

"Why didn't Kaos just Portal it away?" Countdown asked, keeping his eyes on the monster as it came about for another attack.

"Why would he?" asked Glumshanks. "As soon as the dragon appeared, the Book of Power started glowing."

"But it only glows when it's near a segment of the mask," said Wrecking Ball, as the monster began another descent, its furious roar echoing around the forest.

A realization dawned on Stump Smash. "The Bone Dragon is the segment."

"I don't get it," said Flameslinger, still clutching his useless stone bow. "If the dragon is the fragment, then why didn't Kaos stick around?"

"That question has occurred to me,"

Glumshanks said. "I hid behind this bush when the dragon attacked, and ZAP, my legs got frozen. I called for Lord Kaos, but he'd gone. It's not like him at all. Humiliation, yes, abandonment, no—not my Lord Kaos."

The Bone Dragon shrieked as it plunged ever closer.

"Wherever that creep's gotten to, we need to do something about that bag of bones up there," Wrecking Ball urged. "I'm not sure my tongue can lick something that big into shape."

"And my bow's next to useless like this," added Flameslinger.

"Lucky I came along," Countdown said, raising up his arms and firing the rockets that served as his hands. They blasted up into the air, straight toward the Bone Dragon.

"That should do it!" cheered Countdown as the missiles detonated high above them, blossoming into balls of raging fire.

"Then again . . ." the Tech Skylander

added as the Bone Dragon simply swept through the flames.

"Your missiles aren't powerful enough," Flameslinger cried out. "Time to blow your top!"

"I thought you'd never ask," Countdown said with a grin, his eyes already starting to glow a sinister yellow.

"What does that actually mean?" asked Glumshanks, glancing uncertainly from one Skylander to the other.

"Our friend is a real *blast*." Wrecking Ball laughed as the fuse on Countdown's head ignited. The dial on the Tech Skylander's chest spun wildly, and his entire body began to shake.

"Don't lose your heads, guys," Countdown shouted as his own head blasted from his shoulders, shooting toward the Bone Dragon.

"Now I've seen it all," Glumshanks said, dumbstruck as Countdown's head hit the

Bone Dragon in the chest and detonated, sending ribs and bones flying everywhere.

The noise was deafening, and the flash was the brightest the Skylanders had ever seen. Bones rained down from above, the last remains of the terrifying creature.

Glumshanks blinked, glancing over at

the Tech Skylander's body which was already growing a brand-new head.

"That's not even possible," the Troll said in amazement.

"Everything's possible in Skylands," said Flameslinger. "Good going, Countdown!"

"What's Skylands?" Countdown's new head asked, his eyes spinning. "And who's Countdown?"

"He doesn't know?" asked Glumshanks, wincing as a toe bone bounced off his head.

"He loses his memory every time he blows up," Stump Smash explained, narrowly avoiding being impaled by one last rib that slammed into the ground beside him.

"Do I?" asked Countdown.

"Yes," said Flameslinger.

Wrecking Ball said nothing. He was simply looking up to where the dragon had been.

"What's up with him?" asked Countdown. "Whoever he is?"

"Look up there," said the grub, still staring

intently at the sky.

"I don't understand . . ." said Stump Smash, peering up. "What is that?"

Glumshanks stared upward, too. "It looks like a heart."

"A heart made of stone," added Wrecking Ball.

"But it's floating," said Flameslinger. "Why is it . . . ? WHOA!"

The elf ducked as a large bone shot up from where it had embedded itself in the ground. It flew straight toward the strange stone heart, quickly followed by every other bone that had landed on the forest floor.

Before the Skylanders' eyes, the bones came together—reforming the dragon's skeleton, complete with wings, claws, and eyes like glowing coals.

"I know my memory isn't what it could be," said Countdown, "but haven't I seen that thing somewhere before?"

Before anyone could answer, the newly

reformed Bone Dragon roared and dived back toward them.

Chapter Five

Escape!

"What are we going to do?" screamed Glumshanks in a panic.

"What we always do," shouted Flameslinger, starting to run toward Stump Smash. "Win!"

"Need a leg up?" the tree asked, realizing what Flameslinger was planning. The sprinting elf didn't reply, but he leaped up, landing on the mallet that Stump had already dropped to the floor. Stump threw up his arm, propelling his friend into the air. Flameslinger flipped head over burning heels until his feet were pointing straight toward the incoming dragon's head. With a loud *crunch*, Flameslinger's heels smacked into the dragon's skull, knocking it to the side.

The dragon roared, flying off to the right, while Flameslinger tumbled back to the ground and landed gracefully on his feet.

"Okay, I'll admit it," sniffed Glumshanks, "that was pretty impressive."

"We haven't even started." Flameslinger grinned and waved his hands in the air. The Bone Dragon had recomposed itself and was swooping low over the wailing treetops. "That's it, big guy. Catch me if you can."

Flameslinger turned and waited for the dragon to fly into the clearing.

"Get Glumshanks back to the balloon," the elf yelled. "I'm going for a little run."

With that he raced into the trees. The dragon bellowed and flew over the crater, following Flameslinger's smoking path. The rest of the group watched for a moment as the monster blasted the forest with its laser breath, swerving this way and that as it pursued the speedy Skylander.

"Come on," Stump Smash urged, stomping toward Glumshanks. "Flameslinger's fast, but we don't have long."

Glumshanks trembled as the tree raised one of his heavy mallets right above the Troll.

"What are you doing?" Glumshanks squeaked and screwed his eyes tight as Stump brought his hammer-like hands smashing down.

The ground shook with the impact and, when Glumshanks opened his eyes, he saw that the imposing Skylander had just smashed the rock around his petrified feet.

"Stop whimpering and get on my back," Stump Smash instructed him.

"You're going to carry me?"

"Can you walk?"

Glumshanks looked down at his still-solid legs. He shook his head sadly.

"Then what are you waiting for?"

They made their way back to Flynn's airship, while the dragon dived again as it tried to freeze the fleeing Flameslinger.

"I don't w-want to w-worry you," Glumshanks stammered, "but it's coming this way!"

"We're nearly there," shouted Countdown as they cleared the trees. Sure enough, the balloon was already straining at its tethers, Flynn having patched up the basket and prepared for take-off.

"What kept you guys?" he asked, before looking up and spotting the dragon. "Actually, scratch that. I can work it out for myself. Time we weren't here."

"No kidding, Hugo!" said Countdown as he scrambled into the basket, Wrecking Ball bouncing up behind him. "Now get us out of here!"

"Hugo?" Flynn asked.

"He's a little confused," explained Stump Smash as he scrambled up. "He just went boom."

Flynn was already working the controls. "*No problemo*. If we can take off before that

thing gets here, he can call me anything he likes. Except Daphne. I'm definitely not a Daphne."

"Stop babbling and help me aboard," snapped Stump Smash, who was still only halfway into the basket. "These hands were made for clobbering, not climbing."

Flynn and the others grabbed Stump Smash's arms and hauled him into the basket, but Glumshanks lost his grip and tumbled back onto the ground.

The Troll flailed around on his back like an overturned beetle. "I can't stand up!" he wailed. "Help me."

Behind him, Flameslinger burst from the trees and vaulted through the air to land in the basket.

"I suggest we leave," the elf said, panting, as the beat of the Bone Dragon's wings filled the air. "As soon as possible."

"Anchors aweigh," Flynn shouted, releasing the balloon's tethers with a flourish. "Next stop: out of here!"

"Hey, what about me?" yelled Glumshanks. As the balloon rose, a long barbed tongue shot over the edge of the basket, wrapped itself round the Troll's ankle, and pulled him after them.

"Oh the indignity," he moaned as he was dragged through the air upside-down, suspended by Wrecking Ball's tongue. But his whines soon turned to screams of terror when he spotted the Bone Dragon flying straight for them.

"Doesn't this thing ever give up?" shouted Countdown, blasting missiles at the creature, but the dragon swerved in the air, gracefully avoiding every one.

"Don't worry," shouted Flynn. "I recently installed a turbo boost on this baby. Bring on the awesome!" He dramatically flicked a switch—but nothing happened. "Uh-oh!"

"And the awesome is arriving when, exactly?" yelled Stump Smash.

Flynn wiggled the switch until it snapped clean off. "Oops," he said, trying to reconnect it. "I probably should have followed the instructions. Heh. Who knew?"

The dragon zipped by them, battering the balloon in its wake. It turned and rushed back, jaws open wide. Countdown prepared to fire another volley, but it was too late.

The monster's laser breath crackled toward them, hitting the balloon. In a heartbeat, the canvas turned to dense, heavy rock.

Now, there's one thing you need to know

about stone balloons: They don't float. In fact, they do the complete opposite. They fall.

Very fast.

As Flynn's passengers cried out, the now-petrified balloon flipped over and plunged down toward the island, dragging the basket (and Glumshanks) with it.

Chapter Six

The Spotter's Guide

to Hideous & Dangerous Monstrosities

*C*RASH! The stone balloon shattered into a thousand razor-sharp shards as the Skylanders thudded to the ground. Stump Smash groaned and looked up to see the dragon swooping down to finish them off. It opened its mouth, preparing to turn them into stone when . . .

"BUUUUURP!"

A cloud of stinking green mist rushed up to envelop the bony beast. The creature brought itself to a stop, massive wings trying to waft away the foul stench. When it became obvious that nothing could drive away the smell, the dragon turned tail and flew in the opposite direction as fast as it possibly could.

On the ground, Countdown and Flameslinger cheered. Pulling himself back to his feet, Stump Smash turned to see Wrecking Ball looking very pleased with himself.

"Power Belch?" Stump asked, trying not to inhale.

"My best yet," said Wrecking Ball with a smile so wide it nearly split his body in two. "Good thing I ate all those sky-sprouts before we set off. That one's been brewing for a while."

"And people say Trolls are disgusting," grumbled Glumshanks, lying flat on his back and holding his nose.

Flynn sidled up to Stump Smash. "Let's hope that flying boneyard doesn't come back anytime soon." He looked sadly at the broken remains of his beloved balloon. "Even I won't be able to fix this one."

"How are we going to get home?" asked Wrecking Ball. "None of us can fly."

"Then we'd better ask someone who can," said Countdown, pointing his missiles at the sky. He fired off a barrage that exploded high above, the detonations spelling out a message in mile-high letters.

S.O.S.

"Save our Skylanders." Flynn nodded. "You may be a little on the forgetful side, short stuff, but you're one smart bomb. Boom!"

"Thanks, Cali," said Countdown, happily.

Countdown's message worked. They were picked up by Lightning Rod, on his way back from Fantasm Forest. The Storm Titan whipped up a howling gale that blew them all the way back to the Eternal Archive.

The only problem was that the journey got Wrecking Ball so excited that he burped the whole way. He really had eaten a lot of sky-sprouts, and no one could be sure if the Skylanders looked greener than normal due to the unusual transportation or Wrecking Ball's extra gas.

But there was no time to wait for their stomachs to settle. As soon as Hugo heard about the creature from the crater, he hurried off into the depths of the archive. He returned half an hour later, complaining about the Warrior Librarians' indexing system, but clutching a book under his fleshy arm.

"What have you got there, Hugo?" asked Flameslinger as the Mabu gasped for breath.

"It's the Spotter's Guide to Hideous and Dangerous Monstrosities," Hugo said, flashing them a cover that showed a particularly fearsome-looking Fire Viper. "Only the second edition I'm afraid, but I'm sure it'll do."

He led them over to a reading table. "You better bring that appalling bridge-dweller. We might need his help."

The Skylanders followed him, and Flameslinger dragged a chair containing the now securely bound Glumshanks. Petrified legs or not, they weren't taking any chances. Not since Squirmgrub's betrayal.

Hugo slapped the book down on the table and started flipping through the pages. "Now, you said the beast that attacked you was some kind of dragon, correct?"

"Yeah," said Countdown. "But I can't

remember ever seeing one like it before."

Hugo gave the Tech Skylander a withering look. "Can you remember what you had for breakfast this morning?"

"Of course I can," Countdown huffed, sounding annoyed . . . before admitting that he actually couldn't.

"It was new to all of us," Stump Smash said, jumping to Countdown's defense. "Like a gigantic skeleton."

"A dragon made of bone, eh?" said Hugo, turning back to the beginning of the guidebook. "Like this, maybe?"

Flameslinger peeked over Hugo's shoulder. "Yeah, that's it. That's exactly it."

"The Bone Dragon," said Hugo, always happy to drop into an impromptu lecture. "Once, there used to be hundreds of these things, maybe thousands—but they died out centuries ago. They are completely and utterly extinct."

"Except for the one that tried to turn us into

statues," pointed out Flameslinger. "That one looked pretty lively to me."

"It must have been buried beneath the ground," said Wrecking Ball.

"And released when General Disaster detonated his bomb," added Glumshanks. "Does your book say anything about undoing its magic?" The Troll glanced down at his stone legs. "There has to be a way of reversing its laser breath, right?"

Hugo ran a furry finger down the page. "Indeed there is. Those petrified by the Bone Dragon's breath can be returned to flesh and blood by steam from the creature's nostrils."

Flameslinger looked at the rocky weapon he still held in his hand. "I wonder if it works on enchanted bows?" he said sadly.

"And all those trees," Stump Smash added, glaring at Glumshanks. "The ones the Trolls didn't blow up, that is."

"First things first," Hugo said, taking a step closer to the bound Troll. "You're sure

Kaos said the Bone Dragon was the Life fragment?" asked Hugo, peering at the Troll.

"Lord Kaos didn't say much at all," Glumshanks admitted. "He was too busy trying not to get turned to stone."

"But the Book of Power was glowing?" asked Stump Smash.

"Brighter than the Core of Light."

Hugo took off his glasses and wiped them on his jacket. "And there's our problem. Do we try to track down this Bone Dragon or keep searching for Master Eon? Decisions, decisions."

"Sounds to me like they're the same thing," said Countdown.

"Yeah," agreed Wrecking Ball. "If the Bone Dragon is the Life segment of the Mask of Power . . ."

"Kaos won't be far behind," said Flameslinger.

"And Kaos has Master Eon," Countdown concluded.

"What do you think, Stump Smash?" Hugo asked the Life Skylander, but the tree wasn't listening. Instead, he was studying the picture of the Bone Dragon in the book.

"I know my bark's a bit thick at times," he said when he realized they were all looking at him. "But is there something wrong with this picture?"

Flameslinger cast his blindfolded eyes over the drawing. "Don't think so. I'd recognize that thing anywhere. It chased me halfway around the island, remember?"

Stump scratched his chin with a mallet. "I know, but I can't help but think that something is missing."

"That's right," interrupted a voice. "Master Eon and the Book of Power."

Spyro had walked into the library, his eyes

boring into the back of Glumshanks's neck.

"Where is he?" the purple dragon snarled. "Where is Kaos?"

Glumshanks visibly shook as Spyro padded over. "I cannot say," Glumshanks began, his voice wavering. "Lord Kaos—"

"Has crossed a line," said Spyro, smoke curling from his nostrils. "He's gone too far this time."

"I won't tell you where he is," Glumshanks insisted, sticking out his chin in a surprising show of bravado. Perhaps there was more to this Troll than met the eye. "There's nothing you can do to make me betray my master."

Spyro was now snout to nose with the Troll. "Nothing at all?"

Glumshanks shook his head. "No," he squeaked. "Not a thing. There's no point even looking for Kaos. You'll never find him."

"Oh, okay," Spyro said, stepping away. "Fair enough."

Glumshanks's brow furrowed. "Is that it?"

"Well, if you won't tell us," Spyro continued, walking over to the table. "I've been wanting to look at this book of Hugo's anyway."

"You have?" Hugo asked, as mystified as Glumshanks.

"Yup," Spyro confirmed. "Far more interesting than boring old Kaos."

Stump Smash couldn't help but comment. "But, don't we need to find Kaos?" he asked.

Spyro started flicking through the Spotter's Guide. "Nah! It's not like he's important." He paused on a page showing a three-headed serpent. "Ooh, a Hydra. Those are pretty tough."

"Not important?" Glumshanks spluttered. "Lord Kaos is the most important Portal Master in the history of Skylands!"

Spyro thought about this for a minute. "Hmm. Nope, I don't think so. He's not all that." He turned his attention back to the book. "Besides, as you said, there's no point even looking for him. No one cares about him anyway."

"No one cares?" Glumshanks said, not believing his ears. "Well, they should. Okay, so he treats me like dirt—"

"And never says *please* or *thank you*," added Spyro.

"Or gives me a day off."

"Or remembers your birthday."

"But I don't care," Glumshanks snapped. "It's an honor to serve him. Always has been and always will be. He's probably working out how to rescue me right this minute."

Spyro didn't even acknowledge Glumshanks this time. He was too busy reading about two-headed spiders. The Troll was incensed, rocking back and forth in his chair.

"You wait until he's captured the Bone Dragon and taken it back to the Troll Bastion," he ranted. "It's only the beginning. Soon he'll have the remaining segments, and then he'll be heading right back here to rescue me."

A smile played across Spyro's lips. "You're probably right," the dragon said. "What a shame that you're so loyal. A pity that you'd never spill the beans about where he's hiding."

"Never!"

"Like the Troll Bastion."

Glumshanks's face fell.

Spyro turned back to Kaos's lackey. "That is where you said he'd take the Bone Dragon, isn't it?"

"Um," said Glumshanks, realizing his mistake, "I—I could be lying?" he offered, weakly.

"Are you lying, Glumshanks?" Spyro asked quietly.

The Troll looked at his feet. "No," he admitted, no doubt realizing how much trouble he would be in when Kaos got ahold of him. Stone legs would be the least of his problems.

Spyro stalked nearer the Troll. "When I came in, you thought I was going to attack you, didn't you?"

Glumshanks nodded, still not looking up.

"That's what Kaos would have done if the tables were turned, if I were the one tied to that chair."

"He'd point out that you would be—"

"Doomed!" cut in Spyro. "It's lucky for you that I'm not like Kaos. None of us are. We could have finished you off or left you behind, but we're Skylanders. We'd never do that. Master Eon taught us that lesson from day one. Do you understand?"

Glumshanks didn't speak. He just sat there, staring at the floor. Spyro had no idea if his message got through or not—but he had bigger things to worry about right now.

"All right," he said, springing into action. "Flameslinger, come with me. We'll find the Bone Dragon. We can't let Kaos get hold of another segment."

The elf lifted his stone bow. "This won't be much good against the beast."

Spyro placed a paw on the archer's shoulder. "Don't worry. We'll bring the rest of the Skylanders. You can lead the way."

"I'll blaze a trail to the creature," Flameslinger promised. "You can count on me."

"What about us?" asked Countdown. "Should we join you?"

Spyro shook his head. "No. I need you, Stump Smash, and Wrecking Ball to attack Troll Bastion."

"And rescue Master Eon?" the grub asked with a grin.

Spyro nodded. "Think you can manage it with just the three of you?"

Wrecking Ball was already bouncing up and down in anticipation. "I can roll with that!"

"Yeah," Stump Smash agreed, smacking his mallets together at the thought of wading through Troll defenses. "You just leaf it to us."

"You do realize that there are thousands of Trolls in the bastion, don't you?" Glumshanks butted in. "Thousands and thousands of Trolls versus just three Skylanders."

Chapter Seven

Troll Bastion

"So, I drop you fellas off at this Troll Bastion thingy," Flynn said, firing up his brand-new balloon's propeller, "and then pop back when you've saved the old guy, right?"

"Wrong," rumbled Stump Smash, staring ahead intently. The prospect of charging headfirst into a heavily armored Troll castle was the best thing that had happened to him all week!

"Oh yeah," Flynn said, sending a blast of hot air up into the balloon. "I guess Master Eon will be able to Portal you home. You won't need me. You sneak in, and I'll skedaddle back to the archive. Job done."

"That's not exactly how I remember the

plan," admitted Countdown.

"That's hardly surprising, my explosive little buddy," said Flynn, patting Countdown's head before realizing that tapping a live bomb was probably not the best idea he'd ever had.

"That won't work either," Stump Smash said, checking to see if Glumshanks was still dangling from the bottom of the basket in his chair. "The Troll Bastion is a floating fortress. Its walls go right up to the edge of the island. There's nowhere to land."

"So what are you going to do?" Flynn asked. "Jump? If I knew that was the plan I'd have packed some parachutes. I don't usually see the point of them. They just take up space."

"We're going to attack from the air," Stump Smash said, as the Troll Bastion appeared on the horizon. "A frontal assault. No landing. No sneaking. And definitely no skedaddling. Got it?"

Flynn looked at Stump Smash, then at the rapidly approaching fort with its dozens of cannons, catapults and gun turrets, and then at his shiny new balloon.

"Oh well," he finally said, opening the airship's throttle. "No one ever got to be awesome by playing it safe. If you're going to fly into danger, destruction, and other scary things starting with the letter *d*, you might as well do it with Skylands' greatest pilot. Let's do this thing. Boom!"

The balloon shot forward. Glumshanks screamed in terror as every gun on the Trool Bastion locked on to their position.

The battle didn't exactly go as planned. The nearer the balloon got to the bastion, the more guns appeared. They clanked into position along giant oiled tracks. They popped through portholes. They even appeared from the barrels of other guns—which seemed like a bit much, to be honest. The one thing you can say about Trolls is that they never go into battle without being armed to the teeth. In fact, they never go *anywhere* without being armed to the teeth—which is why you can never find any dentists in Skylands.

Before long, Flynn had to swerve the balloon from left to right to avoid cannonballs, missiles, and, strangely, rabbits.

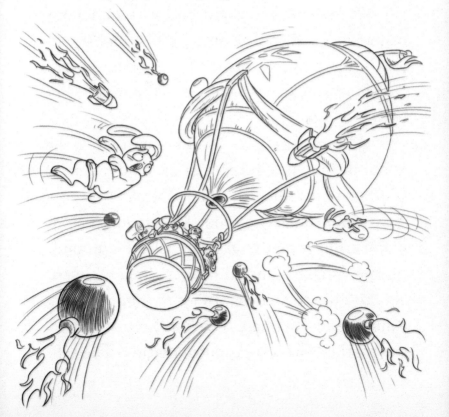

"Who invents a rabbit catapult anyway?" said Flynn as a long-eared projectile whistled over his head.

"Trolls, that's who," replied Stump Smash, whacking an incoming shell with a mallet.

The other Skylanders were just as busy. Countdown was returning fire, sending one hand-missile after another back at the bastion.

Meanwhile, Wrecking Ball was snatching cannonballs out of the air with his tongue and swallowing them, before burping out little clouds of smoke as each one detonated in his belly.

"Mmm, tasty," he commented after gobbling down a fizzing stick of dynamite. "Although it could use a little salt."

Stump Smash spat out a mega nut, before hammering it at the bastion. On the ground, Stump Smash's spiked nuts and acorns were able to take out whole armies of minions with a single shot, but here they hardly even dented the bastion's heavily armored plating. The Life

Skylander snorted in frustration as the nut bounced off the fort with a resounding *clang*.

"We need to get closer if we're ever going to smash our way through," Stump Smash barked. "It's the only way."

"It's the only way to get shot down," Flynn yelled back, jumping to avoid a missile that blasted straight through the basket and out the other side. "I like futile heroic gestures as much as the next guy, but we're not going to do Master Eon any good if we're blown out of the sky."

"Flynn's got a point," Wrecking Ball said, belching on another bomb. "We need a new plan."

"Plans are your department," Flynn said. "My department is keeping us in the air while still appearing funny, debonair, and unbelievably handsome."

"Okay, okay," Stump Smash said, desperate to shut up the pilot for a second so he could think. "I'm sure we'll come up with a plan B if we use our heads!"

Countdown let out an excited laugh. "That's it, Stump Smash! That's exactly what we'll do. You're a genius."

Stump Smash looked at Wrecking Ball and shrugged. "I am?"

Countdown pulled the other Skylanders into a huddle. "This is what we're going to do."

On the bastion, the Trolls were having a whale of a time. The only thing they liked better than trying to blow up somebody was *actually* blowing up somebody. It was in their top five pastimes, along with blowing up bridges, blowing up towns, blowing up islands, and blowing up sheep.

When they weren't blowing up things, they were planning how to blow up things. And when they weren't doing that, they were asleep (and dreaming about blowing up things).

"Hey, I can't believe my luck," said Troll Gunner Blastchops as he emptied more shells from his hideously powerful cannon.

"I know," said Troll Gunner Boomwhiskers from the next turret. "This is the best day of my life!"

Blastchops's green face fell. "Oh no," he groaned.

"What's wrong?"

"The Skylanders' balloon. It's retreating."

Boomwhiskers stared down his sights. "You're right. Now, that is disappointing. I was looking forward to blowing it up."

"Me too," said Blastchops. "Of course, I would have blown it up much betterer."

"No you wouldn't."

"Yes I would."

"No you wouldn't."

"Yes I would."

This kind of thing happened quite a lot at the Troll Bastion. Before long, Blastchops and Boomwhiskers were fighting, trying to insert live sticks of dynamite into each other's ears, nostrils, mouths, and pants.

"Hey!" bellowed a voice from behind. It was Sergeant Slackheap, a particularly ancient and hard-of-hearing Troll, going deaf after years of using dynamite as a cure for earwax. "What's going on?"

Blastchops and Boomwhiskers scrambled to attention, accidentally hitting themselves on their noses with dynamite when they tried to salute.

"Sorry, sir. It was Blastchops," said Boomwhiskers. "He said that you wouldn't know a missile if one dropped on your head."

"I never!" spluttered Blastchops.

"He did, sir!"

"Did not!"

"Did so!"

"Did not!"

"*SIIIIILENCE!*" yelled Slackheap, not that he could hear them anyway. "What's happening with the enemy?"

"They're retreating, sir," reported Boomwhiskers.

"What was that?" asked Slackheap.

"RETREATING!" shouted Blastchops. "You know. Running away. Heading for the hills."

"'Paying their bills'?" Slackheap repeated, getting angrier by the minute. "What are you two talking about? And what's that?"

Blastchops looked where Slackheap was pointing. There, on the battlements, lay an enormous black bomb.

"It's an enormous black bomb," said Boomwhiskers.

"A what?"

"A bomb."

"What did you say?"

"A BOMB, SIR!" yelled Blastchops. "A REALLY BIG BOMB!"

Slackheap tut-tutted. "What do you mean 'I'll ask my mom'? It's an enormous black bomb of course. Any idiot can see that. But where did it come from?"

"No idea," said Boomwhiskers.

"Not a clue," said Blastchops.

"'Right on cue'?" Slackheap said, shaking his head. "You boys speak gibberish. We'd better take it to General Disaster. He's always interested in mysterious explosives that appear under suspicious circumstances. Let's go."

Boomwhiskers and Blastchops followed Sergeant Slackheap into the heart of the Troll Bastion, lugging the enormous black bomb.

"Where did you find this?" the general asked when he set eyes on the explosive— only to raise a hand and stop Slackheap from answering as soon as he saw the look of confusion on the sergeant's wrinkled face. "On second thought, I'll ask the Gunners." General Disaster was actually brighter than you'd expect, especially for a Troll.

"It was lying on the battlements," said Boomwhiskers.

"And it's not one of ours?"

"Nope," said Blastchops.

"So where did it come from?"

"From the Skylanders' balloon," said a voice.

"How do you know that?" asked Boomwhiskers.

"Know what?" said Blastchops, scratching his long nose in puzzlement.

"Know that it came from the balloon," said Boomwhiskers.

"I don't know that."

"But you said."

"Did not."

"Did too."

"Did not."

"Did too."

"Did not."

"Did too."

"Oh, for Arkus's sake," said the voice. "It wasn't him. It was me."

Boomwhiskers and Blastchops both stared

at the enormous black bomb, as did the general. Sergeant Slackheap just stared ahead, having not heard a thing.

"Did that bomb just speak?" the general asked.

"Of course I did," said the bomb, opening its eyes. "And now, if you'll excuse me, I'd like to go boom."

"Boom?" said both Boomwhiskers and Blastchops.

"Yes," replied the bomb. "BOOM!"

The room exploded in a burst of sudden, searing flame.

Chapter Eight

Into the Breach

"**B**OOM!" Flynn cheered as one of the Troll Bastion's walls exploded. "That's what I'm talking about!"

"He did it!" yelled Wrecking Ball.

"Did what?" asked Countdown as a new head magically appeared back on his shoulders.

"You blew up the bastion." Stump Smash chuckled and slapped the Tech Skylander on the back.

"Great!" Countdown said, looking pleased with himself. "Who are you?"

"No time for that now, my concussive companion," interrupted Flynn. "We've got a fortress to storm. Hold on to your missiles. We're going in!"

The pilot slammed down a lever and the balloon's propellers roared into life, rocketing the ship forward. They raced straight for the breach in the bastion's defenses. Desperate Trolls attempted to fire their damaged cannons—only managing to blow themselves up in the process.

"That's it, Flynn," shouted Wrecking Ball as they approached the gap in the walls. "We're nearly there. Keep going."

"No problem," Flynn said, looking up from his controls. "Actually, scratch that. Big problem."

Stump Smash looked toward the bastion. Six walking tanks had stomped into the breach, each pointing a stubby cannon at the balloon.

"Stomper M-fives," Countdown confirmed as the first tank fired off a shot. "Those things are nasty."

Shells started exploding near the balloon.

"That was close," Flynn whimpered. "Too

close. As in any-closer-and-we're-toast close."

"It's fine," grumbled Stump Smash. "We can take it from here. Wrecking Ball?"

The grub leaped into the air. "Give me a hand, Stump Smash."

"I'll give you a *hammer*," replied the Life Skylander, whacking Wrecking Ball with a mallet. He shot over to the bastion, smashing into one of the Stompers.

"Your turn," Stump Smash said, turning to Countdown.

"Here," said the living bomb, pulling off one of his hand-missiles and giving it to the tree. "You'll need this."

"Thanks," Stump Smash said, flipping Countdown over to join Wrecking Ball.

"How are you going to get over there, chief?" Flynn asked, as a Troll mortar exploded dangerously near the balloon.

Stump Smash held Countdown's hand-rocket above his head and grinned.

"Like this!" he yelled as the rocket fired,

propelling him out of the basket and over to the waiting battle.

"Show off," Flynn muttered as he put the balloon in reverse. "You'd never catch me acting like that."

On the bastion, Countdown and Wrecking Ball were seeing off the Stomper M5s as Stump Smash dropped down from the rocket. The missile continued on its way, blasting one of the walking tanks apart. A Mace Major pilot was thrown from its seat, straight toward Stump's waiting mallets.

The Life Skylander brought them together, crushing the Troll. "You've been stumped," he said as the bruised trooper tumbled to the floor.

"I like this place," Wrecking Ball said, rolling beneath a Stomper's legs and bringing it crashing to the ground. "Plenty to damage."

"Don't forget why we're here," Countdown said, blasting the sole remaining Stomper.

"We need to find Eon."

Stump sent a Troll flying out of the hole in the wall. "Then what are we waiting for? Let's go smash!"

"I'm on a roll," Wrecking Ball shouted as he knocked an entire squadron of Trolls from their feet as easily as if they were skittles in a Kangarat bowling alley.

"We must be in the center of the fortress by now," said Countdown, making sure that the Trolls all landed on at least one of his missiles.

"Battering ram!" Stump screamed, knocking a huge dent in the metal door blocking their way. It flew from its hinges, revealing a vast holding bay.

"They've gotta be in here," said Wrecking Ball, finally coming to a halt as Countdown and Stump Smash looked around.

"We'll find 'em," Stump growled. "That's a promise."

"The only thing you'll find is trouble," promised another voice. The Skylanders looked up to see a beastly Troll standing in front of them, glowering at them with one good eye.

"General Disaster," Stump snarled. "If you think you can scare me, you're barking up the wrong tree."

"He's just an old gasbag," said Wrecking Ball, bouncing in front of Stump Smash. "Let me handle this one."

"You?" the general snickered. "A chubby grub? You want to take on the scariest Troll since Captain Trollbeard Braingobbler, the warty pirate chief?"

"That's right," said Wrecking Ball.

"The bravest Troll since Major Bravetroll McCourageous, the champion of the battle of Nightmare Isle?"

"Uh-huh." Wrecking Ball nodded.

"The strongest Troll since Brawnbrain the Mighty, ten-time winner of the Iron Troll of the Year contest?"

"Absolutely," insisted Wrecking Ball.

"Ha! You don't stand a chance, little Skylander," General Disaster jeered. "Not when I'm armed with this." The Troll pulled out a rifle that immediately started to transform—extra muzzles popped out of its chunky barrel, laser sights clicked into place, and inexplicable missile systems swung into view. Before Wrecking Ball could even blink, he was the target of at least two dozen separate missiles and even a few arrows for good measure.

"How do you feel now?" General Disaster said, grinning behind his sights.

"Hungry," said Wrecking Ball, flicking out his tongue. It struck the general in the chest and pulled the Troll, massive gun and all, into the grub's open mouth.

Wrecking Ball swallowed the general whole, burping quietly as his stomach gurgled.

"Mmmmm," he said, licking his lips. "Tastes like

chicken. Time for dessert?"

"I don't think so," shouted Countdown, who had rushed ahead as soon as Wrecking Ball had dispatched the smug soldier. "Look at this."

"What have you found?" asked Stump Smash, who was trudging after the Tech Skylander.

"Not so much *what*," replied Countdown, "as *who*."

He stepped aside to reveal a stone figure.

"Kaos." Wrecking Ball stared at the frozen statue and gasped.

"At least we know why he didn't rescue Glumshanks," said Countdown. "The Bone Dragon turned him to stone."

"And the Book of Power, too," pointed out Wrecking Ball as he spotted the mystical book, which now looked as if it were carved out of rock. It was still held in Squirmgrub's petrified hand. "General Disaster must have brought them back to the bastion."

"At least we've found the book. Maybe we can get the Bone Dragon to turn it back?" wondered Countdown, turning to see Stump Smash looking mournfully into the shadows. "What's up, Stump Smash?"

The tree didn't answer, but merely pointed one of his hammers at the back of the room. Countdown gasped.

There stood a tall, thin statue trapped in a stone cage. It had a long rock beard and was stretching out a hand as if trying to stop something terrible from happening.

"Oh no," said Wrecking Ball, his bottom lip quivering. "Not him!"

Stump Smash nodded as he stared right at the figure. It was worse than they'd imagined. Master Eon has been turned to stone as well.

Chapter Nine

Cornered!

"This is all Kaos's fault," fumed Stump Smash, marching over to the fossilized fiend. "If he hadn't gone after the Bone Dragon, none of this would have happened. The forest, Master Eon—they'd all be okay." He raised his hammer, ready to smash Kaos into pebbles.

"Stump Smash!" Wrecking Ball cried out.

Stump Smash paused, his mallet ready to strike. He glared at Kaos's frozen face, but remembered Spyro's words back at the archive: *"We're Skylanders. We'd never do that. Master Eon taught us that lesson from day one."*

He glanced back at Master Eon, stone eyes staring at him, a hand outstretched. It was as if the old man was pleading with him not to do it.

"We're Skylanders."

Stump Smash let his hammer fall. "We need to get them to the Bone Dragon and persuade him to free them."

Countdown rushed over with a length of coarse rope. "I found this. We could tie them together and tow them from Flynn's balloon."

"It's worth a try," Stump Smash rumbled, giving Kaos one last hard look.

"Where is he?" shouted Countdown as he cleared a path through the Trolls with his missiles. "Where's Flynn?"

Stump Smash looked up at the hole in the bastion wall. All he could see was blue skies. There was no sign of the balloon. Surely he wouldn't have left them here? Not Flynn.

Wrecking Ball belched out a cloud of noxious fumes, reducing the remaining Trolls to a coughing mess. "Perhaps he got shot down?"

Stump Smash continued heaving the frozen forms of Kaos, Squirmgrub, and Master Eon along, the rope they'd tied around the statues over his shoulder. "Then how are we going to get out of here?"

Behind them they could hear the sound of approaching Troll feet. Reinforcements. Soon the Skylanders would be surrounded. And even if they did get off the bastion, they had no idea where to find the Bone Dragon.

"Hey Stump Smash, look at this!" called out Countdown.

Stump Smash joined the living bomb, who was staring at the petrified Book of Power.

"Twist my trunk!" he gasped. "I don't believe it."

Even though the book had been turned to stone, lines were appearing on its pages as if carved by an invisible chisel. Pictures were forming!

"That's the Bone Dragon," Wrecking Ball said, bouncing up and down.

"And a map," said Countdown.

"Not just any map," realized Stump

Smash. "That's the Giggling Forest. The dragon's returning to the crater!"

They could hear the shouts of the Trolls now. The Skylanders turned to see squat shadows moving toward them, light glinting off bazookas, bombs, and even the odd oversize wrench.

"Trouble is, we're still trapped here," grumbled Stump Smash, dropping the rope and putting himself between the statues and the oncoming Trolls.

Wrecking Ball and Countdown dropped into position behind him.

"There's got to be a way," said Countdown.

Behind them, the angry Trolls were still recovering from Wrecking Ball's Power Belch, scrabbling for their weapons.

"There always is," the grub said. "Although, when I get hold of Flynn, remind me to sit on his head."

"That's something I won't forget," said Countdown as the Trolls started firing.

"You'll have to get in line," yelled Stump Smash, whacking a missile back at the Trolls. "Flynn will find out my bark is worse than my bite."

"Well, that's just wonderful," called a familiar voice from behind them. They spun around to see a balloon rising outside the bastion, the pilot grinning lopsidedly at the controls. "You risk your neck to pull off a last-minute rescue . . ."

"Flynn!" cried Wrecking Ball.

"The one and—I'm pleased to say—only," Flynn shouted back. "Sorry about that, fellas. The old girl got a little shook up but, thanks to a little Flynn magic, we're back in business."

"A little shook up, huh?" repeated Stump, a mischievous look passing over his face. "Now, there's an idea. Prepare to get Stump Smashed!"

He raised his hammers high over his head and brought them down hard on the metal floor, sending a shockwave rushing toward the Trolls. The villains were caught in the vibrations, their weapons immediately overloading. As the missile launchers and cannons blew themselves to smithereens, Countdown and Wrecking Ball rushed through the remaining Trolls and leaped into the basket. Stump Smash followed, pulling the stone figures behind him. He clambered aboard the ship, and Flynn fired up the burner. The balloon lifted away from the bastion, Master Eon and the others dangling below the basket next to the still-bound Glumshanks.

"Can't you go any faster?" Stump asked, spitting spiked acorns at the Trolls that were gathering at the breach and desperately trying to rebuild their gun turrets. It wouldn't be long before they were firing again.

The burner roared and the propellers turned, but the balloon barely moved. "It's no good,"

Flynn said. "We're too heavy."

Stump looked over the side of the basket. "It's the statues. They're weighing us down!"

"Could we lose tall, green, and gruesome down there?" asked Flynn, hopefully.

"No!" insisted the Skylanders in unison.

"Phew!" Glumshanks sighed down below.

The Trolls were cackling now, their guns almost ready for action. The balloon had stopped rising. In fact, it was going the other way—dropping back toward the breach.

"Any time you want to do something heroic, just go ahead," prompted Flynn, sweat dripping through his fur. "Don't mind me."

The gun turrets started to crank toward them. Countdown fired off a couple missiles, but they just bounced off the armored plating.

"Seriously," Flynn urged, desperately pumping a lever. "Something awesome would be a very good thing right about now."

Wrecking Ball's stomach rumbled ominously, drawing a look from Countdown.

"Please don't tell me you've got indigestion," he pleaded. "Not now. Not in an enclosed space."

The grub's belly gurgled again. "It must be nerves," he said, before his eyes went wide. "Of course, better out than in!"

"Wrecking Ball," Stump said as the Skylander hopped over to the burner. "What are you doing?"

"Having a gas!"

The Magic grub burped the biggest burp the Skylanders had ever heard. Sickly green vapor burst up into the balloon, inflating it to twice its normal size.

"Way to go!" yelled Flynn as they rocketed into the sky. "I mean, totally gross, but all kinds of awesome. Up, up, and away!"

Below them, the Trolls finally fired their guns, but the shells didn't stand a chance. The balloon was ascending too quickly, the bastion shrinking to a dot in the distance. As Stump and Countdown cheered, Wrecking Ball looked over the edge of the basket and spat a gloop-drenched General Disaster out of his mouth. The Troll tumbled back to join his troops as Flynn steered the airship to safety.

"That's the last time I eat a Troll," Wrecking Ball grinned. "It gave me awful indigestion."

"So where are we heading, amigos?" asked Flynn, giving the burner another blast. "Other than toward inevitable peril, of course."

Stump Smash pushed himself to the front of the basket. "Back to the Giggling Forest," he said grimly. "We're going Bone Dragon hunting."

"Sounds a bit dangerous to me," Flynn said.

"It will be," confirmed Stump.

"Then what are we waiting for?" Flynn grinned, cranking the propellers up to full speed.

Chapter Ten

The Battle in the Crater

"Almost there, guys," said Flynn as he steered the ship around a cloud. "Any ideas on how you're going to persuade the Bone Dragon to unfreeze our stony friends down there?"

"Nope," said Stump Smash.

"So, we're just diving in without a plan?"

"Yup."

"Making it up as we go along with no thought for our own personal safety?"

"Kinda."

Flynn punched the air. "Yahoo! I love it! What could go wrong?"

Wrecking Ball peeked over the side of the basket. "Um . . . that?" he suggested, indicating the scene awaiting them below.

They were approaching the Giggling Forest, zeroing in on General Disaster's giant crater. The place was even more of a mess than the last time. The ground was all churned up into heaps, and thick black smoke was rising from fires that burned unchecked.

"They've really let this place go," said Flynn as he tried to bring them about. With a screech, the Bone Dragon emerged from the smoke, turned around, and dived back down to the battle that was raging in the middle of the crater. Waves of dark energy leaped from the beast's snarling mouth.

Stump Smash spotted a speedy figure on the ground, dodging the dragon's petrifying breath. "It's Flameslinger," he cried, leaping from the basket even though they were still high in the sky. "Look out below!"

The Life Skylander came crashing down

in the middle of the crater just as the Bone
Dragon roared overhead. Countdown and
Wrecking Ball landed close beside him.

"We've told Flynn to stay up high, out of
trouble," panted Countdown.

"That'll be a first," said Wrecking Ball,
turning his attention to the elf. "What's
happening, Sling?"

Flameslinger ran over to them. "It's not
going well," the Fire elf admitted. "He's just
too strong."

"Where's Spyro?" Stump Smash barked. Flameslinger pointed over to a nearby clump of rock. It took Stump a moment to realize *Spyro* was the clump of rock.

"We've thrown everything we've got at it," Flameslinger said. "But it hasn't helped. Everyone's been turned into statues."

Stump Smash glanced over the battlefield, seeing Skylanders frozen where they stood, weapons aloft. Pop Fizz. Sunburn. Bumble Blast. Even Prism Break, who was already made of rock, was lying on his back, completely paralyzed.

"Look out," came a voice from behind. It was Smolderdash, a Fire Skylander. She was rushing over to them, her flame whip cracking behind her. Stump Smash looked up to see the Bone Dragon swooping low toward him. Smolderdash skidded to a halt, an explosive Solar Orb forming in the palm of one hand. The dragon opened its mouth and energy crackled toward the fiery defender. There was a flash of dark light and the monster whooshed overhead. When they looked again, Smolderdash was just another statue, her Solar Orb nothing more than a ball of useless rock.

"Not another one," Flameslinger moaned, shaking his stone bow. "If only I could fire this . . ."

"Uh-oh," said Wrecking Ball, looking up. "The dragon's spotted Flynn." Sure enough, the monster was now heading toward the balloon.

"We need to finish this," said Countdown,

firing missiles toward the creature. One smashed into its neck but did little damage.

"That's it," said Stump Smash. "Get its attention. Fire everything you have at it."

Countdown didn't need to be told twice. "Time for an upgrade," he yelled, as his entire body started shaking. The clock on his chest spun wildly as his hand-missiles grew, doubling their size and then tripling. Before long, they were so heavy it was all Countdown could do to aim them at the creature. "Mega Mortar," he grunted, firing the first missile up into the air. It screamed toward the Bone Dragon, detonating as it met the monster's tail. The bone fragmented, only to immediately start growing back, but the missile had done its work. The dragon's head snapped around, and its glowing eyes focused on the four of them. The monster screamed in fury and changed course, away from Flynn. It was now diving straight for the Skylanders!

"Now, listen up," Stump Smash said. "I've

got a plan." He explained it quickly, never taking his eyes off the dragon.

Moments later, the creature roared and rained laser breath down on them. Stump Smash leaped forward, the blast of energy smashing into the ground behind him.

"Now, Countdown!" he ordered.

The Tech Skylander fired his second Mega Mortar. It shot up to the Bone Dragon, exploding just in front of the creature's face. The dragon shrieked, blinded by the flash, but continued diving toward them.

Countdown didn't stop there. He let loose dozens of missiles that exploded around the dazed dragon, disorientating it even more. It flailed around with its front legs, trying to bat away the explosives, but still continued picking up speed.

"Ready?" Stump Smash asked Wrecking Ball on the ground.

"To *wreck-n-roll*?" the grub replied, leaping into the air. "Always!"

Stump Smash pirouetted on his feet, swinging his hammer and batting Wrecking Ball up toward the stunned dragon. The Magic Skylander smashed through the Bone Dragon's right wing, taking it clear off the monster's body. Then he whipped out his tongue, catching the back of the dragon's bony neck and swinging around to demolish the other wing.

The beast was plummeting faster than the bones could reform. Wrecking Ball hung on to its neck, shrieking with laughter as if he was riding a rollercoaster.

Flameslinger peeked out from his blindfold, looking up at the stricken creature that was now tumbling toward them.

"Um, did any part of your plan involve us getting squashed?" he asked.

"Not so much," yelled Stump. "RUN!"

The Skylanders scattered as the Bone Dragon plowed into the crater, sending up a huge cloud of dust.

Chapter Eleven

Tree-Mendous

Flameslinger didn't wait for the dust to settle. He was off, running in a big circle around and around the crumpled dragon. Within seconds he was traveling so fast that he almost passed himself . . . until he remembered that such a thing was impossible. Behind him, a huge wall of flame rose up from his speeding feet, trapping the Bone Dragon in a circle of fire.

The creature raised its head, still too dazed to react. It tried to petrify the elf, but only managed to freeze parts of the wall of flame surrounding it.

"Stump," Countdown called over to the Life Skylander, as bones started to fly back

toward the monster's massive shoulders. "Its wings are growing back. You need to do it now!"

Stump Smash took a deep breath and coughed out three giant acorns—but they didn't smash into the dragon. Instead, they thudded into the ground beneath its body. The Bone Dragon glanced down at the huge nuts and grinned. Its head whipped around to face the tree and, for the first time, it spoke.

"You'll have to do better than that if you want to beat me," it wheezed in a voice that sounded like shards of rock grating against each other. "You're pathetic."

"Don't worry," Stump replied, squeezing his eyes shut. "I'll grow on you."

Without warning, the Life Skylander thumped his mallet-fists down on the ground. Green sparkling energy flowed across the floor toward the nuts. The acorns began to shake, roots poking through their hard shells.

WHOOMPH!

The nuts expanded into majestic oak trees that pushed themselves through the Bone Dragon's ribcage and newly reformed wings, pinning it to the ground.

The creature bellowed as it tried to escape, but it was caught fast by the wooden branches that came bursting from the thick trunks.

Countdown fired a volley of missiles into the air in celebration as Flameslinger finally skidded to a halt, his flames dying down behind him.

"Whoa," the elf said as he regarded the trapped dragon. "That's impressive. I didn't know you could do that, Stump Smash!"

"Thought it was time I branched out," the tree panted. Exhausted, he plodded over to the dragon's head and rested a hammer on its ivory snout.

"I could give you a splitting headache right now," he growled, staring straight into the Bone Dragon's fiery eyes. "Smash you to pieces. But that's not how we work."

"What do you want from me?" groaned the Bone Dragon, finally giving up its struggle.

Flameslinger approached the monster. "We want you to unfreeze our friends."

"Is that all?" the dragon wheezed. "And then you'll leave me alone?"

"Leave you alone?" Countdown asked, completely bewildered. "You were the one who attacked us! I think."

"Well, of course I did," moaned the dragon. "You'd be crabby, too, if you'd been woken up like that."

"Hang on," said Stump Smash. "Are you saying all this is because the Trolls woke you up?"

"I was having a wonderful dream," the Bone Dragon said wistfully.

"What about?" Stump asked, intrigued.

"Having a snooze," the dragon sighed. "It was fantastic."

"You dream about sleeping?" Flameslinger asked in disbelief. "Isn't that a little weird?"

"Not for me," the dragon explained. "I've always been a lazybones. I love a good nap. In fact, I don't mind a bad nap as long as napping is involved."

"So you weren't trapped underground at all," Stump realized.

"This island is my bed," the dragon yawned. "I must have overslept, because when I woke up an entire forest had grown on top of me."

"What did you do?" asked Countdown.

The dragon tried to shrug but then realized it couldn't, so gave up. "Had forty winks. What else?"

"More like forty thousand," pointed out Stump Smash.

"And then there was an almighty bang, a flash of light and all of a sudden Trolls were firing missiles at me."

"No wonder you were in a bad mood," nodded Stump Smash, glancing at his hammers. "Before I was logged, I liked nothing better than a quick nap. Not for as long as you, of course. I'd only sleep for a few years at a time."

"Sounds heavenly," the Bone Dragon smiled sleepily.

"Okay, then," said Stump Smash, waving for Flynn to start bringing down his frozen cargo. "You return our friends to normal and we'll release you."

"I can get back to sleep?"

"Sure thing," shouted Flynn from the balloon as he lowered the statues of Kaos, Squirmgrub, and Master Eon to the ground. "Looks like you could do with your beauty sleep."

"Not helpful," Countdown snapped at the pilot.

"Sorry!"

"I don't care," said the dragon. "As long as I can get some shut-eye."

"So we have a deal?" asked Stump.

The Bone Dragon didn't reply. Instead,

it took a deep breath and snorted. Steam billowed out across the crater, blocking their view. It was like being in a yeti sauna.

Stump Smash coughed among the hot vapors, but grinned when he heard Flameslinger laugh.

"My bow!" the elf exclaimed, holding his gleaming weapon in the air. "It's gold again."

"That's not all!" Wrecking Ball cheered, bouncing forward to lick a very un-statue-like Spyro.

"Hey, knock it off," said the purple dragon, playfully batting the grub aside. "I'm pleased to see you, too, Wrecks."

Around them, all the other Skylanders had come back to life, stretching as if woken from a deep sleep. A cheer went up from the trees as the steam washed over their leafy brothers and sisters, the sound of laughter filling the Giggling Forest once again.

"How's that?" asked the Bone Dragon, as Stump Smash looked around happily.

"Perfect," the Life Skylander said, beaming. "Just perfect."

"Indeed it is, SKYBLUNDERER!" a weedy voice said with a sneer.

Stump Smash spun around but was knocked off his feet by a bolt of energy.

"Kaos!" Spyro spat as the Skylanders all spun around in unison.

Now freed from the dragon's curse, Kaos was standing, energy crackling around his hands. "Who else wants to taste my Dark Lightning of DOOOOOM?"

He glared at the assembled Skylanders as they stalked toward him.

"Lord Kaos," muttered Glumshanks. His legs were now back to normal, and he looked as if he wanted to use them. "Are you sure this is a good idea? There are an awful lot of them."

"And only one of you," pointed out Stump Smash, whacking his hammers together.

Kaos broke into a roar of hideous laughter.

"That's all I need! Summon my Strength-Sapping Storm of the Darkest Lightning Yet!"

Electricity streamed down from the sky, striking the Skylanders in turn.

"Can't move," wheezed Countdown, as the lightning shorted out his missiles.

"Can't even see," moaned Wrecking Ball.

Stump Smash tried to push himself up, but he couldn't budge. He'd already used some of his own Life force to accelerate the acorns' growth and trap the Bone Dragon. Now, Kaos's infernal light show was sapping what little strength he had left.

"BWA-HA-HAAAAA!" crowed Kaos, watching the Skylanders squirm. "I told you my plan would work!"

"Did you?" Glumshanks asked, looking completely bemused.

"Of course I did, IDIOT!" Kaos squeaked. "Allow the Bone Dragon to turn me to stone so that the Skylosers would capture it for me. It worked perfectly!"

Glumshanks exchanged a look with Squirmgrub. "Did you get the memo on this one?"

The Warrior Librarian shook his mechanical head.

"And now I receive my prize," gloated Kaos, turning his gaze toward the trapped Bone Dragon. "The Life segment is mine! Victory belongs to KAOS!"

Chapter Twelve

The Life Segment

Kaos scampered toward the Bone Dragon, almost dribbling in anticipation. Stump Smash couldn't believe the evil Portal Master had won, after everything they'd gone through.

But hang on! *Master Eon!* Where was Master Eon? Stump Smash glanced over at the cage, but it was smashed to pieces and completely empty.

"Life segment," Kaos boomed at the dragon. "I command you to return to your true form."

"And I command you to STOP THIS."

It all happened so fast. One minute, Kaos's dark lightning was bearing down on them, the next it was gone. Stump Smash looked up to see Kaos standing stock-still, arms outstretched . . . and wearing a look of utter shock.

"Glumshanks!" he screamed. "I can't move! Tell me I haven't been turned to stone again!"

"You haven't," replied the Troll, equally trapped. "It's worse than that."

"What's worse than being turned into a living statue?" Kaos wailed.

"I am," said Master Eon, stepping in front of the tiny Portal Master. The old man towered over

Kaos, the orb at the end of his staff glowing brightly. "You're not the only one who knows a few tricks, you know."

Eon clicked his fingers, and the Book of Power shot out of Squirmgrub's hands, flew over to the old man, and tucked itself beneath his arm. Another *click*, and the Warrior Librarian's armor disintegrated to reveal a very small and very scared-looking bookworm.

"Release me!" commanded Kaos. "I demand that you release me now!"

"So you can steal the Life segment?" Master Eon shook his head. "I don't think so."

"But the Bone Dragon is mine," blustered Kaos, eyes wide with fury.

"The Bone Dragon is not the Life segment," Master Eon announced, his voice echoing around the crater.

Stump Smash stepped up beside his Portal Master, pointing at the Book of Power beneath Eon's arm. "But the book is glowing."

Eon looked down at the book. "Indeed it

is, Stump Smash—but only because it is near something the Bone Dragon has been guarding all these years."

"I don't get it," said Spyro, jumping over to them.

"I assume Hugo showed you a picture of the beast?" Eon said.

"How did you know?" Stump Smash gasped.

"It is what I would have done, and for all his faults Hugo has learned much. But have you, Stump Smash?"

"I . . . I don't understand," Stump Smash said, feeling more than a little lost.

"Look at the Bone Dragon," Master Eon advised. "Look closely. Is there anything that wasn't in the picture?"

Stump Smash turned to study the beast, trying to remember the painting in Hugo's book. The bones were the same, the wings, the stone heart beating in its chest . . .

"Hold on!" Stump exclaimed. "The heart.

It wasn't in the picture. It wasn't there at all."

Eon smiled and turned to the monster. "Because Bone Dragons don't need hearts, do they?"

The dragon nodded. "It was a good-luck charm—or at least it was supposed to be. It's never caused me anything but trouble."

"It was given to you before your slumber?" Eon asked.

"Yes, years ago. I saved a wizard from a Geargolem. He was so grateful, he gave me this stone."

"A stone heart," Stump Smash said quietly. "The opposite of life itself."

Master Eon smiled. "The Life segment of the mask. May I?"

The Bone Dragon looked down at its ribcage. "Will I be left alone if I give it to you?"

Master Eon patted the creature on the snout. "I can ensure you're never disturbed again."

"NOOOO!" screamed Kaos as the elderly Portal Master reached inside the dragon and plucked the heart from between its ribs. "That's mine! If anyone should have the segment it is I, KAOS."

"I can think of no one worse," said Master Eon. The heart glittered in his hand and became a segment of the mask.

"You old FOOL!" spat Kaos. "You think you've won, but I have the other segments. When I find the Fire and Magic pieces, you will feel my wrath. You shall rue the day you ever crossed KAOS. Keep your pathetic segment for now. It's only a matter of time before I get ahold of the next one . . ."

Stump Smash frowned. "What's that supposed to mean?"

Kaos grinned the kind of grin that would make monsters nervous.

"You'll see . . ."

And, with a flash of light, Kaos and his Troll were gone.

"Lord Kaos," squeaked the tiny form of Squirmgrub, backing away from a hungry-looking Wrecking Ball. "You forgot me!"

"I don't think he did," growled Spyro, snatching up the worm. "The Chief Curator wants to have a word with you."

"And our friend wants to get back to sleep," boomed Master Eon. "Everyone, out of the crater. Flynn, you better get clear."

The Skylanders scrambled to the edge of the clearing, Flynn's balloon rising high above them.

Master Eon tapped his staff against the ground and the trees pinning the Bone Dragon vanished, magically transforming into a swarm of butterflies that burst up into the sky. The Bone Dragon sighed happily, stretched his wings, and curled up into a ball.

It was snoring even before Flameslinger had helped Master Eon out of the crater.

"Thank you, my friend," the Portal Master said. "Now, Countdown, we're going to need a rather big explosion . . ."

Chapter Thirteen

Back to Sleep

The Giggling Forest was silenced for a moment as Countdown's head detonated. Earth was thrown up into the air, and the Bone Dragon was buried once and for all.

"Sleep well." Stump Smash nodded as Master Eon rapped his staff against the newly laid ground. Immediately, green shoots poked their way through the forest floor, basking in the sunlight.

"Soon there will be new trees to join the laughter," Master Eon said, smiling. "The Bone Dragon will be able to snooze undisturbed for all eternity."

"And what about the Book of Power?"

Stump Smash asked, glancing at the book tucked under the Portal Master's arm.

"I think we'll take it back to the citadel."

Flameslinger frowned. "Not the Eternal Archive?"

"Squirmgrub has proved that the archive is not as safe as Curator Wiggleworth believed. I think it is time we went home."

"What about Kaos?" asked Stump Smash. "He still has the other segments . . ."

"And will continue to look for the rest," Master Eon agreed. "But we will be ready for him."

The Skylanders cheered and whooped, but Stump Smash thought he saw a hint of worry pass over Master Eon's lined face.

"Master Eon?"

The Portal Master looked down and smiled.

"Don't worry, Stump Smash. There's nothing wrong. I was just wondering what Kaos meant when he spoke of the next segment."

Stump Smash thought back to their

archenemy's ravings.

"It's only a matter of time," Stump repeated, still none the wiser.

"Indeed," said Master Eon, gazing at his celebrating Skylanders. "And that's what worries me . . ."

SKYLANDERS UNIVERSE™

THE MASK OF POWER
ERUPTOR
MEETS THE
NIGHTMARE KING

Chapter One

The Frozen Seas

Anyone who has ever traveled to Skylands knows that it's a magical place. Made up of an infinite number of floating realms, there's an island for everyone. Like sun-drenched golden sands? No problem—head to Blistering Beach. Prefer the dark? Then you'll love Moonlight Mountains. There's even an island where volcanoes spew sweet popcorn high into the sky. Perfect if you're feeling peckish.

Of course, not every island is popular. Take the Frozen Seas, for example. As the name suggests, it's a chilly, unforgiving place. Massive waves of ice hang in the air, frozen in place ever since an everlasting winter fell upon the island millions of years ago. It's so cold that visitors eat ice cream to warm themselves up!

Only people who really, really like the cold go to the Frozen Seas—which is why a Skylander by the name of Eruptor starts this story in a particularly bad mood.

Eruptor is a lava monster, born in the bowels of a volcano. Not the kind that gushes popcorn, but red-hot magma. He's hot-headed in every sense of the word. Scalding lava bubbles beneath his rocky skin, ready to erupt at any moment, and he has a temper to match. Most of the time he keeps his bad moods in check, but he can't help boiling over every now and then. Such as when he's cold—and on this day he was very, very cold.

Eruptor gritted his teeth as he appeared on the top of one of those gigantic frozen waves.

The wind had cut through him as soon as he leaped from a Portal, chilling him to his molten core.

"N-not g-good," he stuttered, teeth chattering like castanets. "N-not g-good at-t-t all!"

"What are you talking about, 'Ruptor?" said the hulking four-armed creature who appeared beside him. "This looks cool to me!"

"That's the problem," snarled Eruptor, turning to face the newcomer. "It's all right for you, Slam Bam. You take an ice bath every night!"

It was true. As a yeti, Slam Bam loved subzero conditions. In fact, before he became a Skylander, he had lived on a floating glacier. He'd spent his days carving ice-sculptures and eating snow cones. His Arctic existence only came to an end when an evil Portal Master known as Kaos blasted Slam Bam's glacier, setting him adrift. Luckily, the yeti washed up on an island that belonged to Master Eon, the greatest Portal Master of them all.

Eon had invited Slam Bam to join the Skylanders, the brave band of heroes who protect Skylands from evil villains like Kaos and his menacing minions. That is how Slam Bam had met Eruptor. Despite their differing temperatures, the two Skylanders became firm friends, united in their fight against the forces of the Darkness.

Slam Bam had always wanted to visit the Frozen Seas, but had never managed to persuade Eruptor to join him—until today. Eon had received a cry for help from the Seas' icy wastes and quickly dispatched the two adventurers to investigate, along with a third Skylander.

"It's fright time!" Grim Creeper announced as he appeared through the Portal, swirling his super-sharp scythe in excitement.

"Hey, watch what you're doing, Grim," chuckled Slam Bam, throwing up two of his arms in fake alarm. "I don't need a haircut."

Grim Creeper grinned. "Sorry, Slam. Just excited to be here."

Eon had come across Grim Creeper after the young ghost saved the prestigious Grim Acres School for Ghost Wrangling. At first, Grim had been turned away from the academy. The Scaremaster in charge thought that the young spirit didn't have what it took to be a reaper. Then, the school was attacked by a gang of galloping ghouls. The other pupils turned and fled in terror, but Grim stood his ground, saving students and teachers alike from the pesky poltergeists. Grim was welcomed into the school and, after he graduated, went on to join the Skylanders. This was his first mission and the Undead Skylander was itching to get started.

"So, what do we do now?" Grim Creeper asked.

"Go home?" Eruptor grumbled.

A look of shock passed over the phantom's face. "You're kidding, right?"

"Of course he is," laughed Slam Bam. "Eruptor never gives up, no matter how much he moans. Ain't that right?" The yeti nudged Eruptor in the ribs, causing the hair on his elbows to sizzle slightly against the lava monster's red-hot hide.

Eruptor couldn't hide a sneaky smile. "Cool it, Slam. I've got a rep to protect!"

Before Slam could reply, a scream sounded across the icy ocean.

"HEEEEEEELP!"

"Sounds like someone's in trouble," Grim Creeper said, clutching his scythe tighter than ever.

"That's why we're here," rumbled Eruptor, peering over the edge of the huge wave. "But how do we get down?"

"We slide!" whooped Slam Bam, throwing himself forward. Grim Creeper's eyes widened as he watched the yeti zoom down the near-vertical drop of the frozen wave, arms outstretched like a surfer.

"That looks like fun," the Undead Skylander said, taking off after Slam Bam. "Come on!"

Eruptor shrugged and leaped into action behind the other two Skylanders. The ice beneath his feet hissed as he picked up speed.

"Last one to the bottom's a popsicle!" he shouted as he steamed past his friends.

What shocking discovery lies in wait for Eruptor? Can Kaos really travel through time? And can the Skylanders track down the next segment of the Mask of Power?

The answers await in . . .

ERUPTOR

MEETS THE NIGHTMARE KING

Also available: